Lieve Baeten

Up and Away with the Little Witch

E
BAE

NorthSouth
New York / London

Lizzy, the Little Witch, had company. Trixie was spending the night. She had brought her favorite fairy-tale book with her, and Lizzy was reading the stories to her.

"'And then the Witch Princess suddenly leaped onto her magic carpet and flew away into the starry night—*wheeeeee!*'"

Lizzy closed the book. "Let's pretend that you are the Witch Princess, Trixie. And I am going to conjure up a flying carpet for you. Pass me my book of spells, please!"

Trixie held the book open while Lizzy chanted,

"Abracadabra, abracaduss,
Carpet, oh, carpet,
Fly away with us!"

"Cat, come back here!
Don't run away!"

"It worked! We're flying!
Hold on tight, Trixie!"

Up and away the carpet sailed, faster than a witch's broomstick, carrying
Lizzy and Trixie off into the night.

On they flew, rising higher and higher. It was perfectly
still up there. Far below they spied a light.

"I wonder what that can be," said Lizzy. "Do you think
there might be something to eat down there? Because I'm
feeling hungry."

"Good evening, Caravan Witch," Lizzy called out. "I'm Lizzy, and this is Trixie the Witch Princess. Do you perchance have something for her to eat?"

"A Witch Princess!" said the Caravan Witch. "What an honor. Come right in! I have something special for you."

"I'll put on a grand performance for the Witch Princess. Complete with drums and trumpets. Then I'll show you my tricks on the flying carpet."

But the Caravan Witch was far too heavy for the flying carpet. "Wait a minute," said Lizzy. "I have my book of spells with me."

"Abracadabra, abracadever, Now this drum is the strongest ever."

Lizzy and the Witch Princess gave the Caravan Witch a big hand.
"Brava! That was wonderful. But now we must continue on our journey. See you again soon!"

Lizzy and Trixie flew on, high over the mountains and above the river.

"Look, there's another light down there!" Trixie shouted.
"The Witch Princess needs to pee."

"Good evening, Boat Witch," said Lizzy. "The little Witch
Princess needs to pee."

"A Witch Princess?" said the Boat Witch. "What an honor!
I have an especially pretty potty for a Witch Princess."

Ooops! There was a frog in the potty! Trixie got such a surprise,
she tumbled right into the river.

The sopping wet Witch Princess was saved!

But both the Witch Princess and the carpet needed to dry out before they could set off again.

"Good night, Boat Witch, and thank you for everything," said Lizzy when Trixie and the carpet were dry. "Now we must continue our journey. See you again soon!"

Once again the carpet rose into the sky. There was almost nothing to be seen down below anymore. The river had disappeared, the road had disappeared, even the moon had disappeared.

"Uh-oh," said Lizzy. "I think we're lost."

"Good evening, you two. Who are you?" said a voice
from up above. "And where are you off to?"
  "I'm Lizzy and this is Trixie the Witch Princess.
We'd like to go home."

"A Witch Princess on board!" said the Balloon Witch. "What an honor."
The Balloon Witch took Lizzy and Trixie home again. They got there
just in time, right before the sun rose—

—bedtime for little witches.